the HIGHEST NUMBER in the WORLD

Roy MacGregor   ILLUSTRATED BY **Geneviève Després**

TUNDRA BOOKS

Text copyright © 2014 by Roy MacGregor
Illustrations copyright © 2014 Geneviève Després

Published in Canada by Tundra Books, a division of Random House of Canada
Limited, One Toronto Street, Suite 300, Toronto, Ontario M5C 2V6

Published in the United States by Tundra Books of Northern New York,
P.O. Box 1030, Plattsburgh, New York 12901

Library of Congress Control Number: 2013940755

Library and Archives Canada Cataloguing in Publication

MacGregor, Roy, 1948–, author
    The highest number in the world / by Roy MacGregor ;
    illustrated by Geneviève Després.

Issued in print and electronic formats.
ISBN 978-1-77049-575-3 (bound).—ISBN 978-1-77049-576-0 (epub)

I. Després, Geneviève, illustrator II. Title.

PS8575.G84H53 2014   jC813'.54   C2013-903531-1
                                                         C2013-903532-X

Edited by Samantha Swenson
Designed by Five Seventeen
The artwork in this book was rendered in gouache.
The type in this book was set in Stempel Schneidler.

Artwork on page 7 by Adam Messier

www.tundrabooks.com

Printed and bound in China

1 2 3 4 5 6   19 18 17 16 15 14

Inspired by Stuart McVittie,
The Bookworm, in Hamilton

To Sadie Rose Cation
— RM

To my husband, my most
entertaining player and coach
— GD

Today, Gabe had made The Spirit, the best hockey team in town.

She was nine and everyone else on The Spirit was ten. But there had never been any doubt that she would make the team.

Even though she was younger than the others, Gabe (who hated being called Gabriella) had worked hard to be able to play at their level. She had even developed a nifty trick of dropping the puck back into her skates to scoot around the defense, and then kicking the puck back up for the shot. Her teammates called the move "The Gabe."

During her tryout, Gabe had worn her lucky number 22 jersey — a Team Canada replica with "Wickenheiser" on the back.

Canadian women's hockey legend Hayley Wickenheiser, an Olympic hero, wore number 22. She'd been Gabe's idol forever — since before Gabe could even pronounce Hayley's long last name!

Gabe's bedroom was a shrine to Hayley, filled with posters, newspaper clippings, magazine articles, hockey cards and a drawing Gabe had made of the two of them — both wearing number 22, of course.

Gabe was counting on getting number 22 with
The Spirit. Some of the other girls called her "Hayley"
to tease her, and even though she pretended to be
bugged, she secretly liked it.

  She'd spent the evening before the tryout
practicing the autographs she'd soon be signing.

  She wrote "Gabe Murray" as carefully as she
could, with a big looping Y at the end.

  And the number 22 neatly dropped into the loop.

Gabe was shaking when Coach Lebrun came into the dressing room with the new Spirit jerseys draped over her arm.

The coach called out the goaltender's name and handed her number 1.

She called out the first defense pairing and handed them numbers 2 and 3.

By the time Coach Lebrun reached the second forward line, Gabe knew what was coming.

"Gabriella Murray," the coach called out, lifting the next jersey off the pile.

"Number 9."

Gabe's heart felt as if a skate had just run across it.

"Are there any other numbers?" Gabe asked the coach afterward.

"They only go to 20," Coach Lebrun said, smiling. "If I had a 22, you'd have it."

Two of the older girls overheard and teased her on the way out.

"Hayley! Number 9! Hayley! Number 9!"

Gabe ran to the washroom, her eyes stinging with tears.

It was the most horrible day of her life.

Gabe buried the number 9 jersey where no one
would ever find it: at the bottom of her closet under
the cardboard boxes filled with her old things. Boxes
holding school pictures of Gabe without her front
teeth, drawings she had done as a baby — and even
her embarrassing first pair of skates, with Velcro
instead of real laces.

Now the jersey was exactly where it belonged.
Buried with all the other stuff Gabe didn't want
anymore.

The worst number in the world.

That night, Gabe's mother sat at the foot of her bed.

"Gabe," she said, "how am I supposed to get your equipment together for your morning practice if you won't tell me where you put your new jersey?"

Gabe buried her face in her pillow.

"I'm not going!"

Gabe's mother shook her head. "Don't you think you're overreacting a bit? It's just a number."

How could she answer that? Her mother couldn't possibly understand.

Gabe couldn't sleep. She flopped around in her bed as if her stuffed animals were body-checking her.

She had scored all her best goals wearing 22. She wore it for luck, even when she wasn't playing hockey. And how could she be like Hayley if she wasn't wearing 22?

22 was her number. She just couldn't play with boring old number 9.

Suddenly light seeped in from the hall. She could see only a silhouette, but that was enough. The mass of curls like steel wool gave her away: Grandma.

No surprise. The grandmother Gabe was named after dropped by almost every day.

"Hi, Gabe," Grandma said, turning on the bedside lamp. She sat on the edge of the bed and set down a big old book. "I hear you got a new hockey sweater."

"Jersey."

"We called them sweaters in my day." Grandma smiled as she picked up the book and opened it to a page filled with old photographs. "Here's a picture of me." She tapped one of the faces in a photograph of a bunched-together hockey team.

"That looks like a boy!" said Gabe.

"I *had* to look like a boy." Grandma laughed. "I hid my hair and called myself Gabe — which I didn't like — but they still caught me."

"*Caught* you?"

"Someone squealed — and they said a girl couldn't play. I wasn't as lucky as you."

"I'm *not* lucky."

"I don't know about that. I hear you got the lucky number."

"No, I didn't," said Gabe. "I got number 9."

"I wore number 9," Grandma said. "Everyone did back then. All the kids in Quebec wanted to be Maurice 'Rocket' Richard. And all the kids everywhere else wanted to be Gordie Howe. They both wore number 9, so the star of every team from peewee to the NHL did too."

Gabe was unconvinced. "No one wears it now."

"Ah," said Grandma, "but maybe there's a very good reason for that."

Gabe scrunched her eyebrows. "What reason?"

"The number's too high."

"The number's too high? What do you mean?" asked Gabe.

"If you want to see number 9 in Montreal," Grandma said, "you have to look up into the rafters."

"Why?" Gabe asked.

"After the Rocket, they didn't want anyone else ever to wear that number again. So they retired it and raised it up to the roof."

"So no one in Montreal can ever wear it again?"
Gabe asked.

Grandma nodded, smiling. "They wouldn't let
me play, so I wore number 9 as a fan and cheered for
all the players who wore 9: The Rocket and Gordie
Howe, but also Teeder Kennedy, Bobby Hull, Andy
Bathgate, Johnny Bucyk and Lanny McDonald. Most
of those number 9s are up in the rafters somewhere
now too."

KURRI
17

GRETZKY
99

K

"Why, even Wayne Gretzky wanted number 9," said Grandma. "When he played junior hockey an older player was already using it, so the coach suggested he double up."

"99," Gabe said quietly.

"Now 99 is up in the rafters with all the others… And now it's time for *you* to get to sleep," Grandma said, turning out the light.

Gabe waited for the door to close, then she flicked the light back on and swung her feet out of bed.

She had something to do.

The next morning, Gabe made her way slowly down the stairs.

She could hear her parents talking.

"She says she isn't going," her mother said. "She's very upset about this jersey."

"I heard her get up," her father said. "I'm sure she'll come around."

Gabe looked down and frowned at the
wrinkles in her new jersey.
Maybe she shouldn't have slept in it.

Gabe was back on the ice, dazzling her new Spirit teammates with "The Gabe" as they practiced.

The wrinkles had all fallen out of number 9. It felt good.

She looked up at the rafters in the little arena. It wasn't high, but high enough.

If they ever raised number 9 to the rafters, she wanted her grandmother standing here with her.

And only one name on the back.

Gabriella.

For both of them.